W9-BYB-916

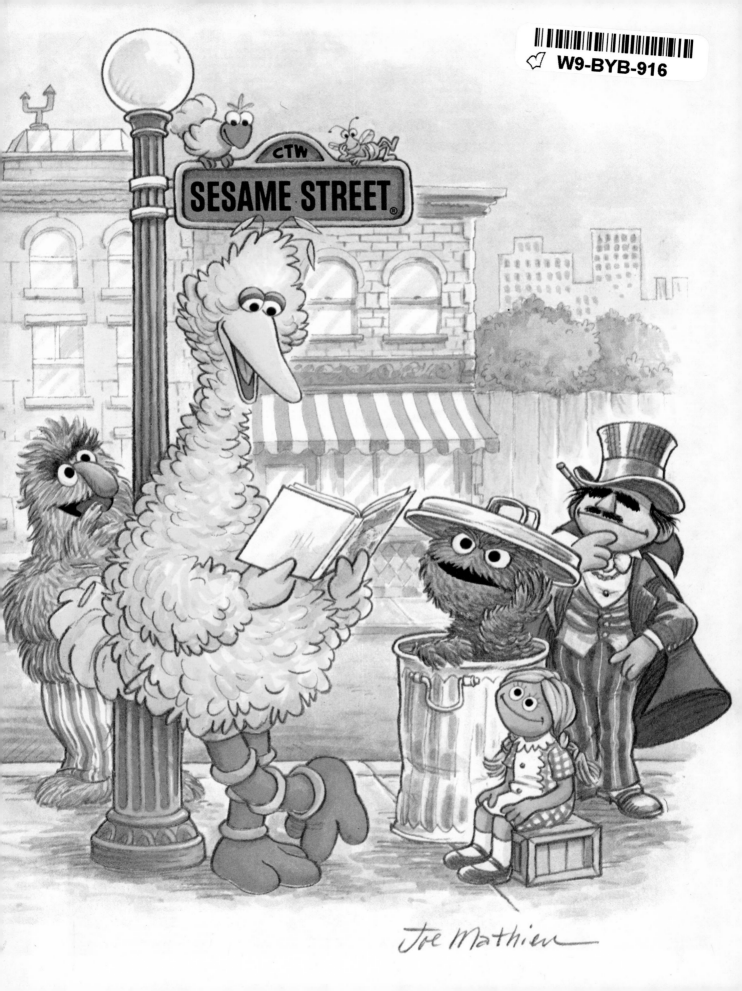

Joe Mathieu

THE SESAME STREET® LIBRARY

With Jim Henson's Muppets

VOLUME 5

FEATURING
THE LETTERS
J AND **K**
AND THE NUMBER
5

Children's Television Workshop/Funk & Wagnalls, Inc.

WRITTEN BY:

Michael Frith
Jerry Juhl
Emily Perl Kingsley
Sharon Lerner
Nina B. Link
Albert G. Miller
Jeffrey Moss
Norman Stiles
Jon Stone
Daniel Wilcox

ILLUSTRATED BY:

Mel Crawford
Peter Cross
Michael Frith
Joseph Mathieu
Harry McNaught
Michael J. Smollin
Bob Taylor
Kay Wood

PHOTOGRAPHS BY:

Charles P. Rowan

Copyright © 1971, 1973, 1974, 1975, 1976, 1977, 1978 by Children's Television Workshop. MUPPET Characters © 1971, 1972, 1973, 1974, 1975, 1976, 1977, 1978 Muppets, Inc. All rights reserved under International and Pan-American Copyright Conventions. ® Sesame Street and the Sesame Street sign are trademarks and servicemarks of Children's Television Workshop. Published in the United States by Random House, Inc., New York, and simultaneously in Canada by Random House of Canada Limited, Toronto, in conjunction with the Children's Television Workshop. Distributed by Funk & Wagnalls, Inc., New York, N.Y. Manufactured in the United States of America.   0-8343-0013-3   1 2 3 4 5 6 7 8 9 0

j J
The Jolly Juggler

There is a jolly juggler
Who juggles every day.
She can juggle lots of things
That all begin with J.

She can juggle jugs and jacks
And jars of jelly, too.
And if your name begins with J
She'll even juggle you.

'Cause she can juggle Johnnies,
And Janes and Joels and Jills.
Ooops, there's been a big mistake—
Hey, wait…my name is Bill!

The Amazing Mumford's Amazing Color Trick

I, the Amazing Mumford, will now perform my AMAZING COLOR TRICK. Watch closely while I pull from this *perfectly empty hat...* something that is red, something that is yellow, something that is blue, and something that is green.

RED 1

YELLOW

BLUE

GREEN

A LA PEANUT BUTTER SANDWICHES!

BLAM!

You see? Red, yellow, blue, and green! Oh, dear! Something seems to have gone wrong in there. I guess you'll have to color them in yourself.

I wonder what happened to all those colors?

Amazing!

Fear not, Penelope! I, the Kindly-Old-Hero-Switch-Operator, will throw this switch and send the train careening off on another track!
That does it, Ernie. As soon as I get untied, I am definitely quitting this story.

Unluckily, a loose crate of bricks fell off the train and onto the railroad tracks, catapulting Penelope up in the air and out to sea.

Unluckily, it was a Pirate Ship, and the Pirates decided to make Penelope walk the plank.

Don't miss how Ernie saves Penelope in Volume 6.

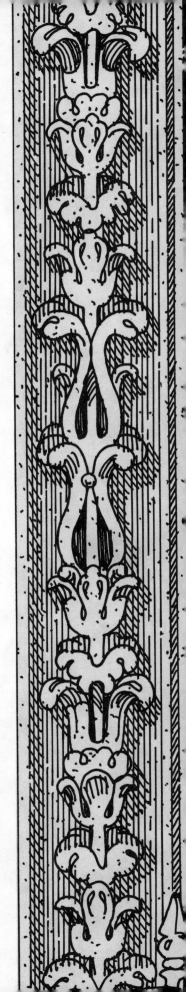

Cinderella

Cinderella was such a pretty girl that her wicked stepmother and stepsisters were jealous of her. They made her dress in rags and do all the housework.

One night the stepmother and her daughters went off to the prince's ball at the palace. Poor Cinderella cried and cried because she had to stay home alone as usual.

Suddenly a lovely lady appeared. "Don't cry," she said. "I am your fairy godmother. I will see that you get to the ball. Just fetch me a pumpkin, four mice, and two lizards."

When the fairy godmother waved her wand, the pumpkin turned into a coach. The mice turned into horses, and the lizards became two footmen. Cinderella found herself bedecked in a beautiful dress and two glass slippers.

"Just remember," warned the godmother. "You must be back by midnight. That is when the magic will end."

Cinderella had such a good time dancing with the prince that she almost forgot what her godmother had told her. When the clock started to strike twelve she had to run out of the palace so fast that she lost one slipper.

But the prince had fallen in love with Cinderella. He sent his men all over the country to find the girl whose foot fit the tiny slipper.

Finally, they came to Cinderella, and, of course, the slipper fit. Cinderella went off to the palace, where she married the prince and lived happily ever after.

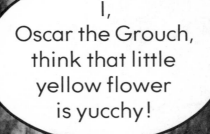

Sam Shows Big Bird Five

Grover's Favorite Color

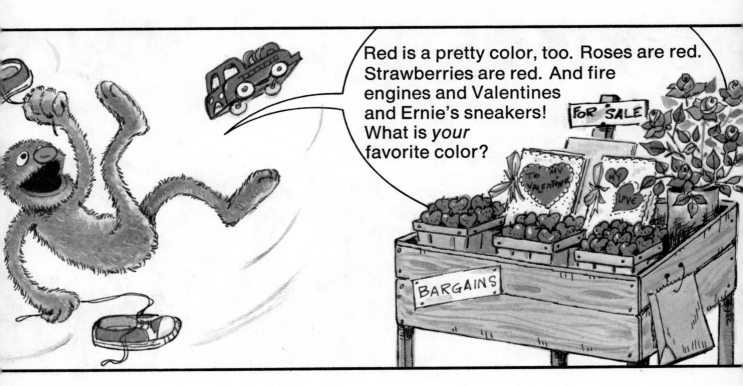

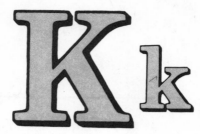

The Pied Kazoo-er of Kamlin

Once upon a time, there was a town named Kamlin. And Kamlin had a problem. Kamlin had too many kangaroos.

Kamlin had kangaroos everywhere. Kangaroos in the kitchens. Kangaroos in the kindergarten. Kangaroos in the keyholes. Uptown, downtown, and midtown, there were kangaroos, kangaroos, kangaroos!

The townspeople couldn't stand it. So they had a town meeting. Mayor Kinkaid made a speech. She said, "We've got too many kangaroos!" And everybody cheered.

Then she said, "We need a plan!" And everybody stopped cheering. Because nobody had a plan. So they all sat there, thinking very hard.

Then up walked a keen-eyed stranger. He was dressed from head to foot in patchwork, and under his arm he carried a long kazoo.

"My friends," he said, "I am the Pied Kazoo-er, and I have the key to your kangaroo problem."

"Are you kidding?" said a townsperson. "How can you solve our kangaroo problem? By playing your kazoo?"

"Yes," said the Pied Kazoo-er, smiling mysteriously, and he raised his kazoo to his lips. Instantly, the air was filled with strange and enchanting music.

Then something magical happened. As the Pied Kazoo-er walked along, playing his kazoo, people began to follow him. All the people on King Street followed him. All the people on Kite Hill followed him. All the people who heard his bewitching music followed him.

In fact, all the people in the whole town of Kamlin followed him. They followed him out of Kamlin to a kingdom far away, where they never saw another kangaroo again.

When the people left, the kangaroos took over the town of Kamlin.
They made it a kangaroo town. It became busy and prosperous, and
soon it was the biggest, most famous kangaroo town in the world.

And the kangaroos lived happily ever after. So did the people.

And, by the way, just in case you didn't notice: Kamlin, and
kangaroo, and kazoo . . . and lots of other words in this story, too . . .
all start with the letter K. It's true. See for yourself.

Tall and Short Poem
by Big Bird and Little Bird

I wish I were as big as you,
I wish that I were tall.
I'm tired of being overlooked,
I'm tired of being small.

If I were tall, I'd stand up straight
And reach the highest shelf,
And if my toy was stuck up there
I could get it by myself!

I wish that I were short like you,
I wish that I were small.
I tower over everyone,
I'm tired of being tall.

If I were short it would be fun,
I'd never bump my head,
And my feet would not get chilly
'Cause they stick out of my bed.

But sometimes when you're trying to hide,
It's better to be small.

And being tall is not so bad
When playing basketball.

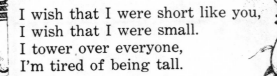

So maybe when we think it out,
What's really best by far
Is finding out what's good about
Being the way you are.

Prince Charming to the Rescue

There is poor, poor Rapunzel. She is trapped in that tower and can't get down. She looks very, very SAD.

Now here I come! Doesn't Rapunzel look HAPPY to see me?

Rapunzel is letting down her long, long hair. She is so EXCITED!

I am climbing up to rescue her. My, I feel so BRAVE.

Now I am letting Rapunzel down. Oh, I feel so PROUD.

There Goes Rapunzel. She is very HAPPY. But now I am trapped in the tower. I am so MAD I could squash a pea!

Sherlock Hemlock in
The Case of the Hidden Squares

I, Sherlock Hemlock, the World's Greatest
Detective, have found 16 squares in this
picture. Can you find that many?
Color them and see.

Ernie and Bert, Firemen

We were really very busy in this book, too, weren't we, Bert?
Ernie